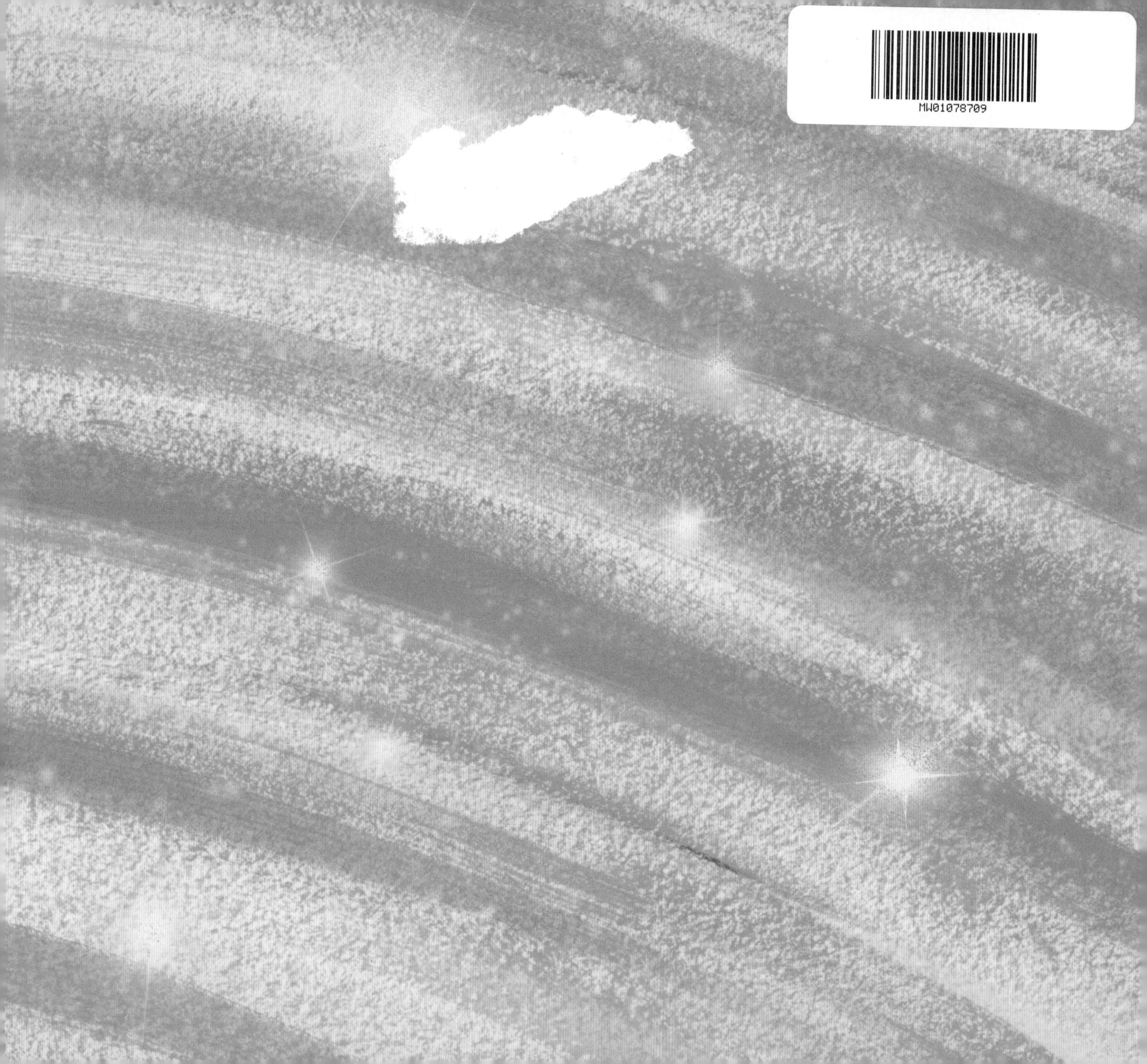
MW01078709

*This book is dedicated to the parents, grandparents, and guardians who work tirelessly to support their families. May your dreams also come true. —K.N.G.*

*To Lyneve and all hardworking mothers with a sweet tooth. —K.Q.*



Book design by Melissa Nelson Greenberg
These images were created using gouache and acrylic on a variety of paper textures combined with Procreate.

Published in 2024 by CAMERON KIDS, an imprint of ABRAMS. 

Library of Congress Cataloging-in-Publication Data available.

ISBN: 978-1-951836-95-5

Printed in China

10 9 8 7 6 5 4 3 2 1

CAMERON KIDS books are available at special discounts when purchased in quantity for premiums and promotions as well as fundraising or educational use. Special editions can also be created to specifications. For details, contact specialsales@abramsbooks.com or the address below.

**ABRAMS** The Art of Books
195 Broadway, New York, NY 10007
abramsbooks.com

# Churro Stand

by KARINA N. GONZÁLEZ

illustrated by KRYSTAL QUILES

cameron kids

¡Crujido!
¡Estallido!

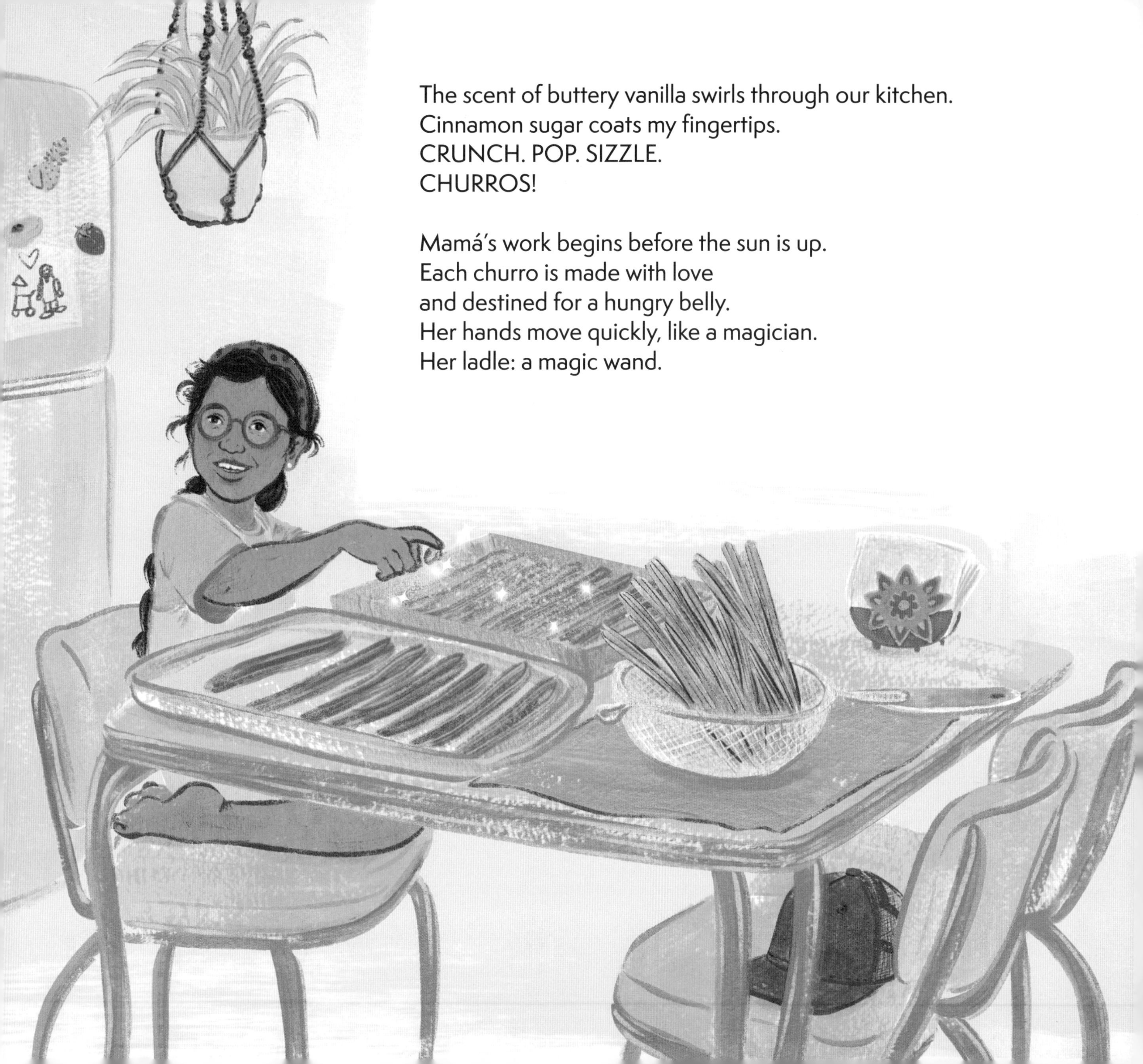

The scent of buttery vanilla swirls through our kitchen.
Cinnamon sugar coats my fingertips.
CRUNCH. POP. SIZZLE.
CHURROS!

Mamá's work begins before the sun is up.
Each churro is made with love
and destined for a hungry belly.
Her hands move quickly, like a magician.
Her ladle: a magic wand.

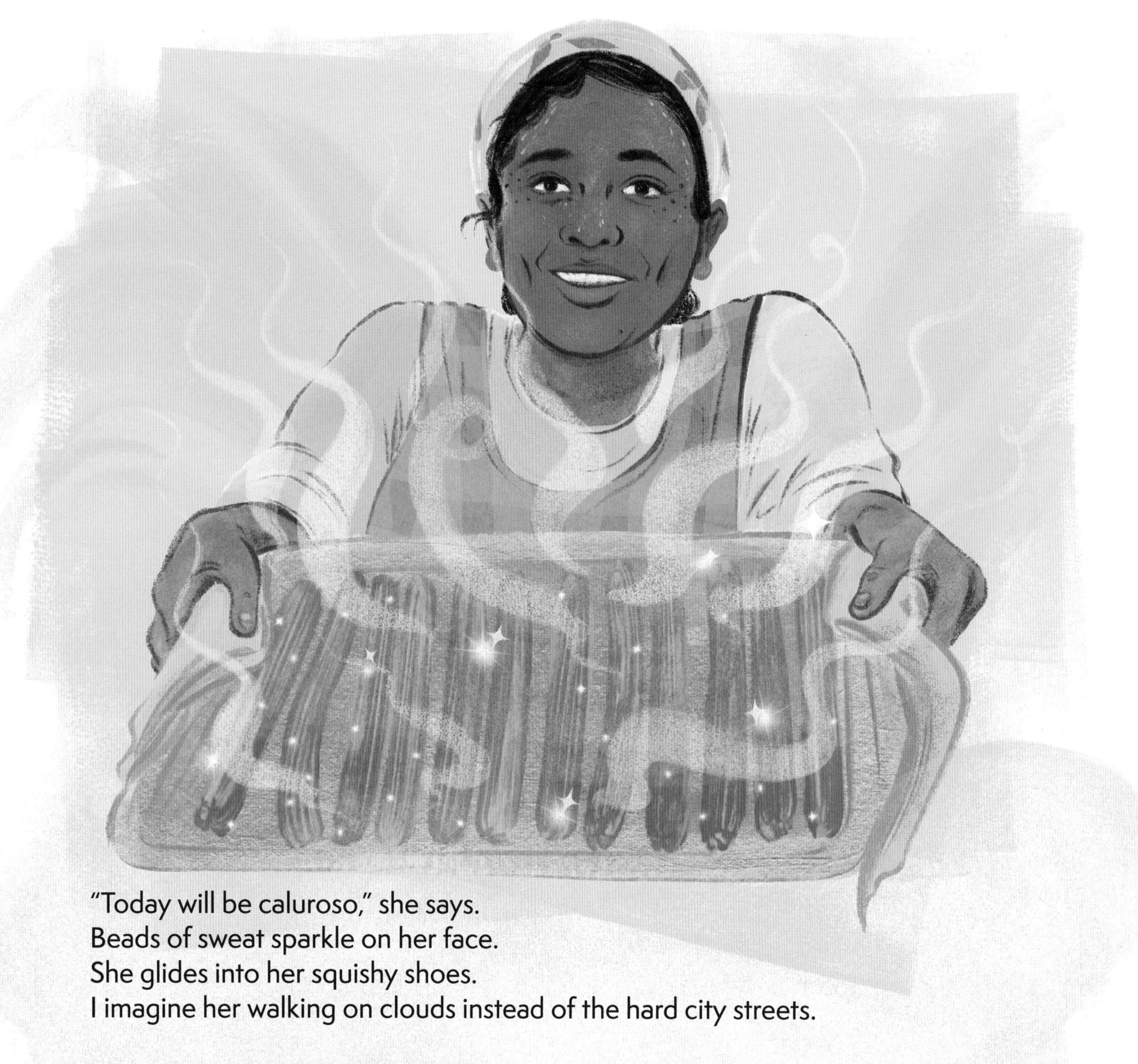

“Today will be caluroso,” she says.
Beads of sweat sparkle on her face.
She glides into her squishy shoes.
I imagine her walking on clouds instead of the hard city streets.

When the churros cool off, Santiago tucks them away.
“Lucía, watch how I do it,” he says.

"Vamos," Mamá beckons.
She rolls out a gigantic suitcase filled with churros—a treasure chest.
Santi carries a basket of napkins and chocolate sauce.
And I cradle our lunch box.

Outside, New York City awakens.
Buses screech and motorcycles ZOOM by.

We rush down the sidewalk and into the dark subway tunnel.
The train races over the East River and into Manhattan.

"This stop is: Union Square."
Finally, we arrive.

Mamá grins as she picks up her pushcart—a shiny, metallic chariot.

Other street vendors are lined up on the sidewalk.

A woman selling ice cream waves our way,
"Hola, Elsa. It's going to be a busy Saturday."

Santi greets an older man selling newspaper,
"Morning, Joon!"

Mamá smiles at a man serving gyros.
"Hi, Tareq. My kids are here today!"
"It's gonna be a hot one!" he responds, handing us each an icy drink.

“What if people don’t want churros?” I ask.
“We should be selling ice cream,” Santi mumbles.

"Everyone loves churros! All around the world," Mamá explains.
"In my pueblo, we call them churros, and in China, they're called yóutiáo!"

We learn that our abuelita Carmen had a churro stand, too.
Mamá's stories transport us to a faraway place that's close to our hearts.
Except there's no avión to take us there, only my imagination and Mamá's memories.

As the morning melts into the afternoon, so does my icy drink.
Sore from standing, Mamá stretches her arms and legs like athletes do.
But people stroll past, hardly noticing her.

The line for ice cream snakes around the corner.
“See?” Santi gestures to the ice cream.
An idea blossoms in my mind.
With chalk, I draw arrows from the subway station to Mamá’s pushcart.
Santi joins in.

One by one, a line of hungry bellies
forms in front of our pushcart.

Santi and I giggle at the faces of the customers as they bite into each ooey-gooey crunchy churro.

Suddenly, a strong breeze flings my hat into the air.

"Ay, no!" Mamá's voice trembles as a RUMBLE echoes through Union Square. Grey clouds crawl over the sky, blocking the summer rays.

Quickly, we gather our supplies and huddle somewhere dry. People hurry indoors, leaving the streets empty and quiet.

CRACK! Lightning flashes, and Mamá checks the time.
"I'm sorry," Santi whispers to Mamá.
The suitcase filled with churros still feels heavy.

After the storm passes, we amble down the soggy sidewalk.
A bell rings from afar and inches closer. DING DING.
Gloria, the ice-cream vendor, pushes her cart next to ours.

"Amiga, ice cream and churros are delicioso—together, we can sell more," Gloria declares.
"Let's do it!" Mamá exclaims.

The line for churro sundaes wraps around the corner.
Mamá and Gloria move in unison, like dancers.
Santi adds the final touch. MMMMMMM!

Frowns magically transform into grins with each bite.
An older man remarks, "Wow—how do you make these ooey-gooey yet somehow crunchy treats?"

"With lots of amor," Mamá giggles.
Her face beams with pride.
For a moment, she's as tall as the surrounding buildings.

“See?” Mamá rejoices. “Everyone loves churros!”

# Author's Note

While on my way home after work, I noticed a mother selling churros inside a Brooklyn subway station with her daughter clutched to her side. In that moment, I saw my mom and me. I remembered accompanying my mother to work on holidays and weekends without understanding that she worked extra hours to pay for my beloved dance classes. Although small in stature, my mother is a *giant* force of positivity in my life and the inspiration of this story. Despite juggling multiple jobs during my childhood, traces of exhaustion on her face were hardly evident. She maintained a steady flow of energy and determination to face the daily demands of life as a mother and underpaid social worker. Here in New York City, I recognize her zeal in the multitude of workers who build the city up and keep bellies full while often going unnoticed and unappreciated. On most city blocks, you will cross paths with a food vendor who is ready to prepare a delicious plate of food or delightful snack for you at an affordable price. In fact, according to the Street Vendor Project, there are more than twenty thousand street vendors[1] in New York City, many of whom work in unsavory working conditions.[2] They stand on their feet for hours at a time on blustery winter days and sweltering summer nights. *Churro Stand* was written to honor the magical heroism of working parents, grandparents, and guardians. May they be celebrated and recognized for their sacrifices. Mami, although I didn't turn out to be a dancer, I hope to move through life as gracefully as you.

# A Call to Action

There are several advocacy groups that are dedicated to educating street vendors about their legal rights while increasing public awareness about the current challenges they face and substantial contributions they provide to our communities.

Several of these organizations are listed below:
**The Street Vendor Project**: An Urban Justice Center advocacy group that works closely with street vendors throughout NYC. www.streetvendor.org
**Inclusive Action for the City**: A Los Angeles–based community-development organization dedicated to uplifting and advocating for low-income communities through economic development initiatives. www.inclusiveaction.org
**StreetNet International**: A worldwide organization committed to promoting an autonomous and democratic alliance of street vendors in fifty countries. www.streetnet.org.za
**Food Chain Workers Alliance**: A coalition of worker-based organizations that organizes to improve wages and working conditions for all workers along the food chain. www.foodchainworkers.org

---

1 The Street Vendor Project

2 Annie Correal, "He Stayed Afloat Selling $3 Tacos. Now He Faces $2,000 in Fines," *New York Times*, August 17, 2021, www.nytimes.com/2021/08/17/nyregion/ny-street-vendors-crackdown.html

# *Glossary*

Abuelita [ah-bweh-**lee**-tah]: grandmother

Amiga [ah-**mee**-gah]: friend

Amor [ah-**mohr**]: love

Aquí [ah-**kee**]: here

Avión [ah-**vyon**]: airplane

Caluroso [kah-loo-**roh**-soh]: very hot

Churro [**choo**-rroh]: a cinnamon sugar–coated, fried tubular pastry popular across Latin America and Spain

Delicioso [deh-lee-**syoh**-soh]: delicious

Hola [**oh**-lah]: greeting meaning "hello"

Pueblo [**pweh**-bloh]: a communal village, town

EVERYONE LOVES CHURROS!